I0699142

K.A. Schultz

Jacob
A Denouement in One Act

K.A. Schultz

Jacob - A Denouement in One Act
by K.A. Schultz
1st edition copyright 2019
2nd edition paperback/Kindle copyright 2023
3rd edition 5 x 8" copyright 2024
Frontispiece crest motif by Adam Oehlers
Lap of a Muse image by K.A. Schultz

ALL RIGHTS RESERVED

Ingram 2025 edition
ISBN 979-8-9894856-9-7

Library of Congress Control Number 2019913858

https://linktr.ee/K.A.Schultz

Also by K.A. Schultz:

PÔÉTÍQUE Dark Poems & Lyric Poetry

KHRYSTMASS Holiday Horror Collection
Short stories & poetry

GÖTHIQUE Ravenscraft Anthology of Horror
Romantically dark horror short stories & poetry

NEITHERIUM Prose & Poetry from the Neither
Elegantly transgressive horror & sci-fi
short stories & poetry

A LETTER FROM KRAMPUS
Interactive book with Krampian video greeting

RUGS ON PUDDLES COATS OVER OCEANS
Collected poems & lyric poetry

Jacob - A Denouement in One Act

By K.A. Schultz

JACOB – *A Denouement in One Act* and its cast of characters was inspired by Charles Dickens' 1843 *A Christmas Carol*; it is also an homage to the author. Any resemblance to actual people, places or events is entirely coincidental. No part of this book or its originating poem, Jacob's recitation (written in 2014, first published at Huffington Post, where the author had an independent blogger account), may be reproduced without the express written consent of K.A. Schultz.

This book includes quotations and references from Charles Dickens' *A Christmas Carol* and from various plays by William Shakespeare, which are cited by name in the text.

This publication will serve as a third edition v.2. It contains a few narrative edits and has been freshly formatted. The second edition contained edits and basic fixes; the third edition was re-formatted from a 6 x 9" volume down to a 5 x 8" size edition. The first edition exists as a cloth-bound, hardback edition, of which 1000 copies were printed. What remains of those are being sold directly by the author.

The author thanks her friend, the late, great, Mary Paul, and acknowledges the creator and members of the *A Christmas Carol* social media fan page on Facebook, for their inspirational stories and posts.

No AI was used in the creation or execution of this work.

To my Husband
Who works tirelessly to provide for all
I also love best
May God Bless This Merry Gentleman

. . . and if you have ever wondered,
"Whatever happened to poor, old Jacob Marley?"
This story is for you, too

TABLE OF CONTENTS

Prologue

Dearest Reader:

Have you ever wondered about poor, old Jacob Marley? I have. For all his epic faults, for all his perennial suffering, I have also thought of Ebenezer Scrooge's old friend as something of an off-sides icon, a sidelined hero.

I was introduced to Charles Dickens' *A Christmas Carol* by way of a gorgeously rendered animated film from 1971, a Chuck Jones produced version which actually won an Oscar for best animated short film in 1972, in which Jacob made his debut as a grotesque, google-eyed apparition directly descended from Dickens' original, first edition illustrations by John Leech. I was creeped out by Marley's face – his jowls hideously agape, his mouth a tooth-filled, black tunnel; his hair and coattails writhing like seaweed. As a bookworm-ish art kid with a penchant for the darkly imaginative, I was thoroughly spooked – and hooked.

Decades later, having read a number of Dickens' works, and having collected *A Christmas Carol* in myriad forms – from annotated tomes to pop-up picture books, and having watched countless versions of *Carol* put to screen – my love of this classic tale and fixation on whom I believe to be the saddest apparition to ever walk the face of the Earth have now led me to recollect, compile and put to print a few notable, written items, for myself and anyone else who may ever have asked:

Whatever happened to poor, old Jacob Marley?

Seven years' suffering, were, it appears, only the beginning of an eternity of lonesome subsistence for Marley's ghost in *A Christmas Carol*. I felt that Jacob Marley's plight begged for some exposition, as did the sources of his internal conflicts warrant imaginary exploration: Marley had contributed to society in the practical sense; he had been a law-abiding, productive citizen. He'd also been a steadfast business partner, and not just any friend, but a loyal one, to a highly significant other. It would seem a life path like Marley's should not lead to only an endless and lamentable purgatory, as implied in *Carol*.

But it was charity, of the literal and figurative kind, Dickens sought to spotlight, so he created Jacob as a static narrative trigger, the very personification of charity's unmitigated absence. Marley's character was denied any iota of a *joie de vivre* in life, nor was he granted a postmortem redemptive resolution. Jacob was merely resurrected – and decrepitly so – to serve as tragic interventionist for Ebenezer Scrooge's legendary salvation in life.

In *A Christmas Carol*, Jacob's opportunities were over and done with. The first words are, after all, "Marley was dead." There was, is, no pity for Jacob, not even the slightest inkling of a potential deliverance for him. All Jacob could muster was to leave the proverbial window wide open for Scrooge to attain that which he did not, could not, would never. . .

∞ ♥ ∞

How wonderful, then, that while a college student studying abroad in Europe, a slender, hand-bound volume would place itself into my unsuspecting but welcoming hands!

Whether this find was a meant-to-be for this lit-loving writer, or just dumb luck, is perhaps not mine to over-think or over-own. If the Spirits of all untold Rest-of-the-Stories were entrusting me with the task of providing a dog-eared set of pages some safe harbor for eventual transcription of its contents so that Jacob Marley could, like his compatriot, Ebenezer Scrooge, have at long last some opportunity for resolution, I humbly accept now, as I did back then, this most remarkable and singular assignment.

And if you share *any* of these sentimentalities about Jacob, the results of my efforts are here, for you too, as well.

To best illustrate how my project, this book, came about, and to keep everything at its most comprehensible, allow me to list what follows:

First, are my diary entries, intended to set the stage for my story within a story, so to speak.

Next, follows the actual *Jacob – A Denouement in One Act*. The *Denouement*, the found booklet I mentioned above, is mostly in dialogue. It is formatted like a script, as if for a play, perhaps for some performance, like a mummery. Have you heard of those?

Mummeries were brief and often fantastical, folkish plays, popular in earlier centuries, tapped as pre-tech pastimes at all levels of society. Amateur at-home performances took place in palace theaters and bedsheet-curtained sitting rooms alike, where preparation and rehearsals provided days, if not weeks, of activity for friends and family. You may recall the opening scene of Louisa May Alcott's *Little Women*, where the sisters re-enact their annual Christmas-time performance of *A Pilgrim's Progress* as one of the best-known literary examples of Victorian theater-at-home.

Finally, I will share an alternate chapter – or stave, as it were – of *Jacob – A Denouement in One Act*, along with the transcription of a video recording my husband made on a Christmas morning over 10 years ago, to help explain something that remains inexplicable to me to this day as regards the antique booklet itself. For you see, the *Denouement* is no longer in my possession.

I will always wonder if I served simply as random recipient of a lucky coincidence in the finding of Jacob's Denouement, or if it was intended to enter into my quite nice but conventional world for some reason I don't yet know, outside of its immediately presenting itself to me as a labor of love task, for me to bring it to this point – here in print – for you to now read, as much as its being something from which my very soul benefited. As Mary Shelley put it in *Frankenstein,* another classic on par with *Carol*, I was, am, *inspirited.*

I also wonder on the timing of this project. I wonder if the *Denouement* stayed forgotten and packed away for so many years, so that I would have the opportunity to rediscover, transcribe, and publish it at specifically this point in time, so to leave me, us, with some positive take-way in an era where we all might need most its embedded message – that of *forgiveness*.

As much as Dickens' *A Christmas Carol* inspired in its readers a new social awareness – charity, spiked with equal parts cheer – his evolutionary narrative was all about opportunity created by deeds done by one wiser and thusly evolved, as embodied in the "new" Scrooge. This *Denouement* looks back to address *retroactive* atonement, which does, indeed, require forgiveness.

Forgiveness is not only reliant on the domino effect of the old plus the new, but also on the sum total as *inspired by one and carried forward by another*.

The *Denouement*, like its predecessor, does account most wonderfully for that most inevitable of ingredients, Human Nature. We all err; and to be sure, Scrooge and Marley were pros. But Jacob, stuck as his old, miserable self in *Carol*, remained not only in need of forgiveness of those he may have wronged in life; he was in dire need of the understanding that he could forgive *himself*.

Jacob – A Denouement in One Act also invokes something profound, tied directly in with this age of over-information, which, despite all appearances of constant and grand-scale connectivity, has the unfortunate tendency to categorize, factionalize, and ultimately divide us.

We are pitted against each other over endless minutiae, when, in fact, there is so much more we have in common, so much more to celebrate as is, which can be explored, individually and collectively, as we evolve, organically and over time. Much of the disconnect exists because forgiveness these days, from grand scale dramatic reunions to the by-the-way shrugging off of all the little irritants we encounter and engender, is in decidedly short supply. Jacob serves as a fresh reminder that even the smallest connections, borne of words or deeds and their intention, have immensely transformative power – in any dimension.

Punitive destinies, bah humbug!

The aforementioned college year abroad was in Germany, where I spent two semesters at the University of Hamburg. In addition to my Art History classes, I attended undergraduate Liberal Arts courses, one being a seminar on Martin Luther. One particular philosophical aspect of his, I embraced as a mantra for life, what I perceive to be central to his notable legacy as the pre-eminent working Man's theologian. Let me put it in this way; it is a simple math:

We are the sums of our deeds.

We are ourselves equations to which we add for the duration of our lives – taking away, borrowing, and then adding back to (including exponentially!) who we are by all we do – and all we don't. Might have beens matter, too. And those abstracted non-deeds? Here is where I circle back to Jacob Marley's character: I believe they are summed up in precisely that which haunted Jacob: *Regret*. Regret as stoked by one's inability to do, or undo as it concerned him, in both his former life and present state. Jacob in *A Christmas Carol* is mired – positively drowning – in Futility amidst Regret, rendering him stagnant, and therefore regrettably, passively, so.

Jacob – A Denouement in One Act, on the other hand, opens wide a new door to resolution, as being a ripple effect sparked by past deeds, not dead-end concluded. Like smooth stones well cast, I do believe that one's deeds can skip over waves of Time and Place, to catch up and find their source, and to make that much-needed splash somewhere down the winding paths of All Things Possible.

While the *Denouement* turns a few, big things quite on their heads, it taps, like its venerated predecessor did in droves a Dickensian otherworldliness for purely transcendental, theatrical effect, leaving us now with both: a much-loved, classic tale and its magical, mystical offshoot, to spook and delight us as they work in tandem to deliver most welcoming messages of forgiveness and redemption. How cool is that?

Finding the Denouement

Ages ago, in what feels like another life – pre-kids, pre-career, pre-work and more work – I was a college student spending my junior undergraduate year in Germany at the *Universität Hamburg*. During that year, I had the good fortune to travel throughout much of Europe, living and learning in the way only students seem to manage it, with that enviable, penniless panache that has hallmarked the world of *Studentium*: nickel plate riches, with no more ballast than what fits a small backpack.

Between semesters, I took a train trip, circumnavigating the country, with Berlin as my *Endstation*. While there, I rented a room at a romantically ramshackle youth hostel. From my fourth-floor window, I could see the majestic dome of the *Charlottenburger Schloss,* aglow at the beginning and end of each day. Beyond that stretched an endless cityscape, a skyline peppered with quaintly variegated rooflines, vertically hatched at random intervals by old church spires and regal clock towers, and also by brightly colored, towering construction cranes, the city being in high, post-reunification construction mode.

It was during my winter season sojourn there that I happened upon an antique, cloth-bound booklet that was entitled, *Jacob – A Denouement in One Act.*

Having always been a compulsive chronicler, I kept diaries as a little girl and throughout college. To this day, I maintain paper day-planners alongside my technology into which workaday notes, thoughts, facts, events, and schedules are entered. The entries keep my thoughts straight. They prioritize and remind me as obligations and time accrue and fly at ever faster rates (Personal Relativity?). Likewise, they can jog my memory in a flash. At a glance, I can see what the weather was on a given day, what outfit I wore where, what I made for dinner, or, say, at which well-child checkup one of my children would have received some vaccination, and even how well (or not) they had braved the needle. Little things, big things, happy and sad things have been logged for decades.

A few pages in a couple of old planners are missing, removed intentionally, where perhaps something may have been put to pen, best removed, being intended only for me, for the experience or lesson granted, not posterity. I suppose it would at some point be wise to use them for kindling.

How grateful I am, that I still at least have my diary from back then, to be able to read now my scribblings, as to what happened while in Berlin.

The entries that follow, which I happily share despite their personal nature, will best explain the origins of the antique book called JACOB. They have been taken verbatim from the journal I was keeping at the time. Allow the dated notations and contemporaneous comments to convey aspects of this story that, given what happened years late, baffle me to this day. Perhaps an explanation of the *whole* story is not even mine to offer, not my responsibility, as it were, as mere conveyer of an anonymous other's work. . .

The picture I hope to paint by sharing the *Denouement* and its backstory is one of *Zauber*, magic the dog-eared novella revealed to me, which has stayed with me through the years, through thick and thin, through loves and life, and all the wonderfulness anyone could ever extract from the ordinary.

If "faith" is to believe what one cannot see, then I default to grateful participation in the generous motivation of the book's unidentified writer – one haunted, you could say, by the Spirit of Good Intent, which exists to point us in the True North directions we *ought* to go, should *want* to go.

I do believe *Jacob – A Denouement in One Act* was gifted to remind me, us, of all the Good that was – and still is – out there.

Smartphone calendaring to spiral bound day-planners, going then all the way back to the leather-clad, key-lock diaries I would hide under my bed as a girl, then onto the slim journals that would travel with me as I began to venture out, into the world. . .

Here are my entries:

Dec. 15

It's Midnight and I am beat.

My Art History paper, done already—so inspired by all the awesome stuff I am seeing! It'll be ready to print and turn in once I get back to the 'Uni' in Hamburg. Relieve. It'll be a great head start on the second semester German Masters class. Oral presentation should go well too, though I know I'm going to be sooo nervous, doing it all in 'Deutsch.' Hans Baldung Grien (was this guy an eccentric genius or what?)—I mean, how can anyone, knowing what we know today, ever really get past the nuts n bolts of the iconography of his day? Sure, to know the definition of something is to know the thing, I guess, but to really GET it? I'm trying. But, I did come here to study, and to see his and so many others' awesome works in person. There's nothing like standing in front of the real deal, so many great works of art, and soaking it up, inch by inch, detail by detail. And so what if they teased me for asking for a letter grade (Germans don't do grades at this level, the way our schools do it) for credit back home. It's ok. 'Herr Dr Prof' assured me I was well on my way to getting a "1"—an A—for the first semester. Yay!

Tomorrow, I'm granting myself the day to 'bummel,' browse n shop til my student-level (as in meager) funds are gone. Need gifts and maybe find a little something just for me— something commemorative, maybe vintage, or antique, from one of the stalls out by Poet's Square to take back home—a 'Mitbringsel' to represent these weeks in Berlin. What a city. . .

Need to mention: This time of year, the sun is super low all day, and it's pitch black by 5. So, it's been dark as night for hours. The days being this short, makes everything feel, well, twilight-like. More time for candles, for ghosts and spooky tales.... The dark falls instantly, like a light switch being turned off. Keeps reminding me just how far north I am on this globe...

So tired. To bed now! But it's just started to snow. The first real snow, and the city's transformation in the last hour has been magical—Christmas-y, sugar-sifted 'Lebkuchen' magic. I hate to end my day despite this walking corpse weariness I feel— I could just sit here and look out the window forever...

I'm procrastinating by writing all this, can you tell? I wish I had a camera that could take a panoramic night photo. Berlin looks like something right out of a fairy tale. Everything is outlined in white, like a reverse etching—glowing, shadowed, then highlighted with a painterly precision, like those moody snowscapes by my absolute fave, Caspar David Friedrich. Saw a few of his works today, something I've looked forward to for so long. Hauntingly gorgeous, those ruins, the ancient oaks... What is dead? What is dormant? These works make me ask, make me wonder... In the stillness of winter, do these things merge?

Now, even the Palace looks asleep—'Gute Nacht,' Sophie-Charlotte! I won't push til dawn (yawning!). It's freaking freezing over here by the window, and the panes are now totally frosted over. Under the covers, girl—now!

Dec.16

What a cold day, but so beautiful outside! My new-old coat, which I found at that consignment shop on Schleuter Strasse, serves me well, even if it's over-sized. Warm with a capital W.

Stopped in at my new favorite antiques booth, the one right at the entrance to the Poet's Square. Rummaged around a bit in the bin next to the kiosk where the new stuff gets tossed til priced. The old man, so nice, was not there—such a bummer; he gave me the best discount on my tea kettle. Today, it was a young guy, one of those lanky Berliner types with bangs over his eyes, tattered, mis-matched clothes, looking so (how do I put it?) euro-cool, like no American can do it. He ignored me, just read his book, sold books n stuff to others, basically left me alone as I dug around in the huge, wooden box.

Well, I found an old folio. Over-sized, stained, the pages as soft as fabric. The gorgeous postcard mounted onto the cover practically justified the buy all by itself. The pic's of a Christmas Market, somewhere in London, I think, as it can't be anything but Big Ben in the background So, how'd it make its way here? Instead of a proper binding, the sheets are (sort of) secured with big stitches which once connected them to a fabric spine. The whole thing's neatly tied up with a wide, brown ribbon (gold or yellow back in its day?). Confession (sort of): I did something kind of sneaky. Stuck inside the folio, which contained gorgeous pages of sheet music, some of them carols I recognized, there was a book. Just wedged in between two pages. Small, also poorly bound, homemade looking, with a fabric cover in super-faded green. The raggedy book is called "Jacob—A Denouement in One Act." Ok. So it's a script(?). There is a wreath-like motif on its cover—pretty. Well, I left the booklet inside the folio (where I will swear it had been all along!). I didn't do anything, or say anything, I just handed over the folio and asked the guy to quote me a price. 5 Euro, he said. OK. So, I paid for the book(s!) and left. I think that dog-eared, little book was supposed to go home (well to the hostel) with me. You know, like a puppy. I'll put it to bed and I will love it and care for it—promise!

Dec.17

Gotta run, but—update—yes, the story is a script, and it's about Jacob, as in Jacob Marley! Scrooge's Marley! Did I already say it is in English? Well, it is, and in an older English-speak, m'lady. A tad dated, but loverly. I can just hear the voices, like from some way-back place in time. . .

So, but for the terrible condition of the book (the pages are frail, and they smell kinda musty—yuck), it's legible. I will have to store the book in wrapping just to hold it together.

At least from what I can decipher so far—some I might have to guess as I go—I'll be able to read it ok, no problem. Nice that it's in me native tongue, matey, tho a smidge olde worlde.

What I need to do, is transcribe the text, save it as an electric document, which will be a terrific project for whenever I can find myself a nice chunk of free and quiet hours. Whenever— ha! Who am I kidding? I hereby promise to get a roundtuit for ye olde project transcription. "The Jacob Project." How nice, to have my new laptop computer for this kind of work. Sure, it beats the desk unit, and it most definitely beasts that sweet ol' baby blue Smith-Corona Mom and Dad gave me when I turned eight, which, though that thing had miles of sentences on it, was nothing compared to these lil machines with memory we now have.

Dec.20

Been too busy. Will write more soon. Quickly: Here's the inscription in Jacob. When I saw it, I nearly fell out of my chair:

Dedication For you, my dearest little Nikki,
Who thought to ask,
"Whatever happened to poor, old Jacob Marley?"
A Denouement in One Act
So that you may better sleep,
Duly consoled,
Through any long winter's night.

C.

No kidding—I almost felt queasy when I saw the "C". How fun to imagine the possibilities. I'll do some research— maybe it can serve as the basis of my someday master's thesis? I'm sure I could merge an art historical theme with a lit twist. And being mostly a ghost story—so much fun—with that element of mysticism, the book does seem to possess the power to have found ME, just as I feel I was meant to have it. So, I might as well do something solid with it. For it.

Dec.22

Was feeling guilty about the spare book find thing. Went back yesterday to the Poet's Square with my Jacob book, thinking I would explain how I "sort of accidentally" came to have it and to then offer to pay something for the book itself.

I also really wanted to ask the old man what he might know about the origins of that batch of stuff in the box anyway. Turns out, he wasn't there—again—but the lanky Berliner was. Again. Sooo—well, we talked about it. He was really nice, even surprised I had come back with the book. Said he loved my accent ;) and then he old me the book was mine to care for, and that, considering the shape it was in, it was the book's good fortune to have found me. See? He <u>also</u> said the book found me!

And guess what? I wound up spending the entire afternoon at the booth—hanging out, talking with the guy, even helping out with a couple sales. Told him I could at least "earn" some portion of my new acquisition—that made him laugh, which was about when I realized how cute he was. Couldn't believe it when it started to get dark; it was actually kind of embarrassing to realize how long I had been hanging out there!

Confession: Yep, ok, I was stalling. I was reluctant to exit the scenario, ya know? Did not want to say 'ciao' to this guy (they don't say 'Tschüss' so much here; they say 'ciao'). As he closed up, the Lanky B asked if I wanted to join him for a beer at a 'Kneipe' nearby, this half-timbered nook with stained glass windows, which I had literally sketched just the other day (planning to do a pen and ink drawing of it soon). I said in my most casual n cool 'Deutsch-Student' tone, "Ja, sicher. . ."

Well. . . he's in the kitchen right now, making 'Kaffee,' and it's the next day, which is now. Smiling. Ciao for now!

∞ ♥ ∞

I graduated from college with a double major in Art History and German, but I never got my master's degree; the need for a solid paycheck took me onto other career paths, all esoteric plans set aside in favor of the practical.

Nor did the lanky Berliner and I stay in touch, though I still smile when I think back on our days together. He was a music student, a gifted musician at that. So, the sheet music in the folio I gave to him. The small, old book that I netted from that experience, for all my excitement over the find, was sidelined in the name of short-term romantic fixation, and was, I confess, too easily shelved, and then soon completely forgotten. In the normal course of travel and, well, life – packing and unpacking, moving back to campus at State University and then packing it all up again after graduation – it was absorbed in with the rest of my college memorabilia and eventually stored away along with my textbooks, sketchbooks, and binders. The box containing my Poet's Square souvenir sat undisturbed on a closet shelf at my parent's home for years, quietly relegated to my youthful past.

Years, later, after my youngest, our daughter, began preschool, my mother and I resolved to sort through the contents of my childhood bedroom, the plan being to move the vintage suite of furniture to my new home, for my little girl to use. A few additional boxes of books were added at the last moment to the truckload, and so the novella also, finally, made its way home with me.

Some years after that, I was laid off from work. Finding myself with something I hadn't had in forever – a patch of free time and all of it to myself – I decided to make the best of it and to tackle the transcription of *Jacob*. Finally.

And so, the result of those quiet, solitary hours I spent with that frail, little volume – a gift, really, in retrospect – follows.

I look back on my immersion into *Jacob – A Denouement in One Act* with fondness. It is almost with a feeling of longing, to "go there" again, for the story took me on what felt like a metaphysical journey as I transposed the words of the dialogue, letter for letter to a working document. But that kind of creative trip is not possible, for the transcription put here to print is the result of my single, one and done, read-through.

At night, when the household was asleep, I would sit in the kitchen at the table, sometimes sipping on a glass of wine, as I would read and decipher the text. I would enter dialogue into my laptop straight into the early morning hours, so absorbed was I. The condition of some of the pages made for slow and thoughtful interpretation. A few of the pages were stuck to each other, and difficult to separate, making the mottled text even harder to read. But the imagery that put itself together, what played out in my mind as I read and typed the dialogue, remains with me as the loveliest of memories, like a play I might have seen ages ago, as a child. Though distant and dream-like, certain moments in this play, and a few points in its narrative – a few scenes, a handful of particularly lyrical lines – remain crystal clear.

Was *Jacob* intended for the stage, perhaps a mummery? It's possible, for the way the text was formatted. But no such play, titled the same or similarly, was ever produced, at least not professionally, to the extent my research has shown me.

Was anyone other than "little Nikki" familiar with the story? Did anyone (else) even read the novella? That question remains unanswered, for the book suggests its having been a one-off, created and given to "Nikki" as a personal gift. It had no real cover, and its binding was rudimentary and rather poorly done.

A few primitive illustrations had been glued onto blank pages in between the Staves, or chapters, but they were extremely faded, and in places, torn clean off. Part of the illustration for this edition, I commissioned. It is based on what little the artist could discern of the original frontspiece, which yes indeed, does resemble its historic counterpart, its "part one," as it were. The figure within the crest is from an ink drawing I created whilst studying overseas, a veiled figure I call my dark Muse. And while the script to *Jacob – A Denouement in One Act* might in due time prove to be an amazing literary artifact, it was, for the years it was in my possession, a rather quaintly mysterious, but decidedly homemade glimpse into an unknown someone's past.

I thank God, the Fates, and the Spirits, for the lone opportunity I was granted to read *Jacob*, and that I at least saw fit to record the text as I read it. More on that at the conclusion of this book. . .

And that one draft, it now being safely housed electronically and here in these pages, can at least continue to exist of its own accord. Although I am no credentialed scholar, I do hope that my literary transcription and the book's backstory – how it came into my possession – will entertain you, and that its narrative will satisfy your musings and concerns as to our Man of the Hour, Mr. Jacob Marley, and what, evidently, became of him.

To the extent the eyes and ears from times Past, Present, and Yet to Come are indeed (still) among us, I thank *Jacob's* author – whoever they may be – for letting me serve as archivist, docent, and ardent admirer.

Enjoy.

Jacob

A Denouement in One Act

Dedication

For you, my dearest little Nikki,
Who thought to ask,
"Whatever happened to poor, old
Jacob Marley?"
A Denouement in One Act
So that you may better sleep,
Duly consoled,
Through any long winter's night

C.

CAST OF CHARACTERS

JACOB MARLEY

DR. TIM CRATCHIT

BOB CRATCHIT

EBENEZER SCROOGE

CAST/CHORUS: Men, women, and children who will enact the Christmas Day dinner scene at the home of Bob Cratchit from *A Christmas Carol* and the Tim Cratchit life scenes, and who populate the winter solstice street scene at the conclusion of "Stave Final"

Introduction

(SCENE: The curtain rises on the closing scene of Charles Dickens' A Christmas Carol. Surrounded by celebrating Cratchit family members, a jubilant Ebenezer Scrooge takes Tiny Tim up, into his arms. Carolers wander about to depict old London city street activities, reciting the closing lines of the Dickens story, as taken from the original text)

CAST
(Alternating)
Scrooge was better than his word . . .

He did it all, and infinitely more; and to Tiny Tim, who did NOT die, he was a second father . . . He became as good a friend, as good a master, and as good a man, as the good old city knew . . .

Some people laughed to see the alteration in him, but he let them laugh, and little heeded them; for he was wise enough to know that nothing ever happened on this globe, for good, at which some people did not have their fill of laughter in the outset . . .

His own heart laughed; and that was quite enough for him . . .

. . . and it was always said of him, that he knew how to keep Christmas well . . .

. . . and so, as Tiny Tim, observed, God bless us, Everyone!

(Lights fade to black. As the curtain lowers, one cast member, elegantly dressed and poised, extracts himself from the chorus and approaches the audience. He is, as yet unknown to the audience, the adult Tim Cratchit)

TIM:
. . . better than his word . . . you know the story.

You, dear participants, are here to listen and revisit, as the Spirits did back then and will doubtless do again—when least expected, but most needed—to this great tale.

You are here to honor and invite back into your own hearts a story so known and loved it has woven itself into the very fabric of our lives. What illuminates today, as it did back then, the darkest slice of a midnight hour, is no doubt what also brought you here, before me now.

When night outweighs the day and Time's passages are steeped in cold, Man yearns for that which invokes warmth and light. And love.

What we seek comes in many forms, be it a liberating truth, a restful solitude, or some small instance in which the giving supersedes the taking. Indeed, good want places me here, before you, as well, to introduce a small aside, a denouement if you will, of something intended to shed light upon what I warrant not a few of you have at some point asked:

What about poor, old Jacob Marley?

(As Tim recedes and is swallowed in shadow, he concludes)

Let once more the whispering shivers and ghostly specters haunt us onto a better path! As we aspire to what is best in all of us, let us employ, for a second time, the dark to illustrate the light.

(Lights come up to illuminate a room)

There. Look upon Jacob Marley, who yes, indeed, was, is dead. Dead as a doornail.

(Tim exits)

Stave I

(SCENE: A compact room, both a bedchamber and an office. Monochromatic, in shades of blue and gray, the space is dimly and mysteriously lit to evoke a never-ending night, a standstill of time. The only light comes from a lamp situated upon a desk. Coins are stacked upon the desk. There is a fireplace, but no fire. There is a daybed, rendered so as to appear comfortless and unsleepable. Tattered curtains hang at the window. There is an ornate and massive wardrobe with double doors at center stage. Rubbish is strewn upon the floor. The room's entry door is at stage right. Behind the stage left wall, there is a void, cloaked in darkness.

The door opens, slowly, smoothly, and without any sound. A vastly tall apparition dressed all in black, with a hood covering the head, and face shrouded, slowly, smoothly enters, as if afloat. It carries a scythe. This is the Ghost of Christmas Yet to Come. The Ghost reaches the center of the room. Suddenly, the ghost's regal, stiff, and stealthy posture collapses into one of slumped-over weariness. As the hood falls, we see a rudimentary scaffold, like the prop of a puppeteer. As the robe is shrugged off, we see an old man, pale, with long hair, dressed in yet another costume, featuring a garishly cheerful dress shirt and vest of crimson and deep green. A sprig of holly appears to be pinned to the vest; perhaps, it is not a boutonnière, but instead, a stake of holly, pierced through his chest, its topmost leaves and berries splayed over the lapel. This is the costume of the Ghost of Christmas Present.

The old man was, is, dressed up as both ghosts; that he still wears most of the second ensemble suggests he had no time to change completely out of the red and green costume for his next role. A matching, luxurious coat of green velvet is heaped upon the floor, as if tossed aside in a hurry; it is part of the costume of the Ghost of Christmas Present.

The old man lifts the black robe, now puddled about him, and walks wearily to the wardrobe, dragging it behind him. He gathers the velvet coat into his arms as well. As he nears the closet, the doors slowly swing open in unison on their own, further suggesting otherworldly powers. Artful illumination lights the interior of the wardrobe. Another costume hangs within the wardrobe. It is a white gown, luminous, but as if lit from within. A pair of wings hangs next to the gown, as does a tattered, white wig. An unlit torch is propped up to one side. This is the costume of the Ghost of Christmas Past.

The old man hangs the Christmas Yet to Come robe upon a hook in the wardrobe; he lays the green coat onto the floor of the closet, and stashes additional items—black boots, a black face cloth, the scythe.

The man next shrugs off the rest of the Christmas Present costume, which reveals yet one more ensemble, having been worn underneath the previous layer: It is a decrepit, faded, and molded suit, now recognizable in the context of the previous Spirit reveals, as that worn by Jacob Marley when he paid his lamentation visit to Ebenezer Scrooge.

The old man steps into a pair of weathered shoes, next removing a tattered and dirty, white folded kerchief from another hook in the closet. Looping the fabric under his chin, the man secures it at the top of his head, resituating a horrifically slackened, but rigid, creaking jaw.

He takes a pair of shackles from the closet floor and fastens one around each ankle. The old man next lumbers to a large travel trunk, the ankle bracelets clanking. From the trunk, he removes a length of chain from which padlocks hang, like charms on a bracelet. The last links of the chain are never fully removed from the trunk, suggesting infinite length stored within. The man threads and hooks the chain to his shackles, grimacing, his hands at his lower back as he straightens up. A section of chain he loops up and clips to his belt. He is now tethered at numerous points. Henceforward, the old man makes a great show of struggling with these chains with every move.

The man is Jacob Marley. It was he alone who, in magically rendered costume, enacted every ghostly apparition who visited Ebenezer Scrooge on that fateful Christmas Eve. This set of performances was Jacob's task upon his visit to Earth: For one night only, he was to try and save his friend, spare Scrooge from a fate similar to his own.

Having completed his four visitations, Jacob has now returned, exhausted, to the dismal room that is his solitary purgatory, there to resume his penance, which is to count his coins, over and over again)

JACOB:
(Inhales deeply, overcome, and begins to cry—wailingly, broken heartedly—and then to speak, as he commences with his activities)

"How now?" How now, indeed!

My task is done!

Or is it?

A lifetime in one night—a lifetime in three hours! What light and life I gazed back upon in the smallest of slivers granted me, and how dark the black now beckons in contrast! Oh, the agony! Oh, the void!

Dreariness and silence, my only companions, they tug at my wretched soul. And this splinter that pierces what in life was once my heart, it is now nothing more than a pinion that marks a most lonesome infinity. What, I must ask, have I crafted?

This room is my prison, a torture chamber, reserved for only the most selfish of architects.

Oh, I demanded, loud and clear, and the Fates, those baleful sisters, they listened and granted as much—an isolation that makes mockery of solitude and solace!

They gave me what I wanted, what I in my life's course so charted. But, to suffer it forever and in this fashion? (Jacob trails off, wailing, crying) Aye, three hours, three crumbs stolen from the manna served at Mankind's banquet! Three hours in which I was made witness to all from which my lone friend might one day be deprived, as I myself have hungered . . .

(Wailing)

Friend! 'twas but a name for like-minded scoundrels in communion with each other! What lone title bestowed upon two cantankerous men, co-joined? And what did I know of "friend"? Could I have imagined, the only links I would forge would be these damnable iron ties? They slink like vipers at my ankles and waist, binding me to this space . . . . . . aye, wisdom's bitterest apple is to know the taste of all Might Have Been's and Should Have Been's, a dour zest, indeed! And a chance of redemptive course? Ha! I cast that aside as I plotted. I sailed as I assailed . . .

And now, I am left with this wrenching echo, which would twist my gut, had I yet a gut to twist. Still, it somehow manages to gnaw ceaselessly in the depths of this hollow carcass, and goodness, it leaves me famished. . . .

(Jacob pats his belly)

But the absence of knowing—what did I accomplish? It is but a penance upon penance! Did the grand task of my visitations upon old Eb do their work? In life, the Fates held wide the drapes of opportunity and allowed me to pass through, unfettered in my ambitions. They watched, dispassionate, as I, the deprived dreamer, became instead the most ruthless of lenders.

The sisters were seated in silence long before that, as my father, in ignorance, presumed prosperity would alleviate the thespian predilections and eccentric inclinations of a son he would never understand.

Not the first of men to err as paternal guide, the father trained his son to wield wealth like the sharpest of swords. A stage was built, but from which neither sonnet nor story were to be delivered. 'twas a perch from which percentages and penalties were promulgated with the bombast of an enterprising divo! Not rich was I, though possessor indeed of vast legal tender . . .

Funds I finagled to deprive others of their inconsequential security, not only to build my accounts but to finance the eventual takeover of my very own mentor . . . And where did it land me? I am left poorer than any debtor in prison. I have Want for companionship and Ignorance as my advisor . . . wicked urchins; they claw at my shirttails even now . . .

(Looking behind and around him, as if these beings lurk close by)

I understand and see too well. I know not only what I wrought in life but more so what I left in its wake. So, in this pathetic place I must remain, blind to the transformative effects of my endeavors of one night. Aye, my former cohort cried with fear and writhed with remorse, most divinely demonstrated; but do I not know as an actor the risk of suspicious exuberance? To have seen passionate demonstration, promises, and contrition is as likely to have seen a co-conspirator at his Shakespearean best! (Bitterly, paraphrasing Shakespeare, from *As You Like It*) All the world's a stage . . .

And this apparition in his time did indeed play many parts. Ha! The question lies in what follows, when the curtains are drawn and no audience is nigh, when no applause exists to foster the doling out of generous good will. What is said or left unsaid when the onlookers are gone home? What is achieved when exchanges of gratitude or adulation are not at hand?

What is Man—and what is Ebenezer—capable of, if reward is not placed on some near shelf, there to shine and magnify . . . and further tempt him?

(Lamenting, to the universe)

Man, how great, yet how paltry and selfish a servant you are. Gods and monarchs, crooks and rakes, our commonality as drying human husks reduces us until at last we are equal in dust with each other. Back, back into the soil we go! When moved no more by invisible puppet strings of Fate, Free Will, and Destiny, when no more tied to the very crossed beams that housed both a Savior and a thief; pray tell, what are we?

(Jacob pauses to consider his words, shaking his head in sadness)

Ignorance, you are the victor and as such shall remain my master. Another stretch of chain, one more padlock hooked to my weary wrists . . . . . . so heavy . . . nowhere to go, nowhere to fly, nowhere else to be . . . Alone but for the one night granted me, to sail amongst the earth-bound poltergeists, and find my way through the alleys of a city, to the wasted chambers of one familiar to me above all others . . .

(Jacob cries out in agony)

Scrooge! The name, it pains my bones to speak it! (Jacob shuffles over to his desk. The wardrobe doors close themselves) And so, I am left, bereft. This is my nether-worldly space; my one assigned task. My gold . . .

My old, cold coins of gold . . .

Damned bits and pieces, unfeeling tokens . . . indeed, I reaped for which in life I toiled. . . and now I pay eternal price, alone, oh so, alone . . .

My God, I pray Eb listened. Hades, I pray he learned. Sisters, I pray he fights against your ropes and hides well your intrepid shears. Cut him not off too quickly. May he yet un-build what in life I never did, what now chains me to this hell of my own making . . . Oh, Jacob Marley, you fool . . . back to work you go . . .

(Jacob seats himself, arranges his chains, and takes up his one task. He begins to count his coins)

One thousand one, one thousand two
Better for me than low-born you.
One thousand three, one thousand four . . .
If the pithy monk can do this,
Every hour in obeisance bent,
Then any man can do it and any man so should.
And when he does, and done is did,
And as a doornail is fulfilled,
He can yet find rank
Amongst scoundrels, cads, and kings . . .
. . . one thousand five, one thousand six . . .
When nothing's broken, what's to fix? . . .
One thousand seven, one thousand eight . . .
Oh Midas, sir, I replicate . . .
One thousand nine, one thousand ten . . .
Oh, foolish, merry gentlemen!

. . . one thousand eleven . . .
Out of sight is out of mind . . .
One thousand twelve . . .
The smallest coin, the miser tithes . . .
Thirteen, fourteen . . .
With blinders on . . .
Fifteen and then sixteen . . .
To lock myself within these walls . . .
Avowed to keep prosperity
For only, only, only me! . . .
Seventeen and eighteen . . .
As I played so I must pray; my penance paid, full price .
. .
Nineteen, now is twenty . . .

(Jacob will have at this point stacked the coins, or placed them on a scale or some such device; but then, he dumps the coins back into a heap on his desk and begins stacking them again, reciting the poem once more, from the beginning)

One thousand one, one thousand two . . .
Better for me . . . (etcetera)

(The light fades. Jacob's voice trails off as he recites and counts)

End, Stave I

Stave II

(SCENE: Time passes—years of time. This will be illustrated by lighting, visual cues, and trick effects. Perhaps a clock's hands begin to spin around, slow at first, then faster. Perhaps the clock's face glows with a palpitating luminosity, like a heartbeat. Jacob is seen always at his desk, always stacking the same set of coins, as the light comes up and fades to dark in irregular intervals. Perhaps, at one moment of illumination, his coat is on; soon after, it is back off again. At points of re-illumination, more cobwebs will have appeared, which seem to grow ever longer, thicker, and more covered in dust. Presently, a faint light appears in the corner of the one window, moving to suggest a glowing object approaching. The light comes to shine underneath Jacob's door. A loud, echo-filled knock sounds. Jacob, in the midst of yet another count, is visibly startled)

TIM:
(Calling through the closed door)
Jacob! Jacob Marley!

JACOB:
What, heh?

(Realizing someone is at the door)

Who goes there? If you are the devil himself, you are excused! Begone, stranger, my hell is generously furnished! Have I not paid enough to stave off further visitations from the likes of you?

TIM:
No, no! There is no Luciferian entity at your door, but neither is it a seraphic messenger. Open the door, sir; you will see.

JACOB:
What reason is there for me to expect other than more dark and dank, however personified, to slink about my stoop, at best to throw my way another 70 years' solitary servitude?

TIM:
For once, please, trust. Trust what you hear and what you will soon see.

JACOB:
(To himself)
The irony escapes me not, for both in life and after death did I rely upon costumed deceit. 'twas but an eye's blink hence, that I portrayed a trio of spirits for one who still walked among men, whose end remains a mystery. Oh, but the illogical fear that visits me now!

Fear!
How such an old emotion could be renewed in me, peculiar to one so long ago swept away and left to wallow in futile longing for anything that might pass for a heart? Oh, distant God in your far-off heaven, protect this empty carcass!

May I not at least be spared a doubly gifted damnation?

(Jacob leaves his desk and shuffles to the door, wringing his clasped hands, stumbling over the chains that drag behind him. As he nears the door, it slowly swings open of its own accord. There stands a regal, old man, dressed and coifed so as to suggest a gentleman from an era, decades into the future from the ghostly Christmas Eve visitations of A Christmas Carol. *It is the recently deceased Tim Cratchit. He is carrying a lantern)*

TIM:
Fear me not, Jacob Marley!

JACOB:
(Falling to his knees)
I am weak victim to the vestigial remains of a conscience that walked too long ago. I fall upon my knees—I can no longer hold ground. I am a fully broken and lonely old shade.

TIM:
(Stepping through the door, he sets the lantern down, reaches out for Jacob's hand and takes it. This touch lifts Jacob smoothly to his feet)
Come, stand up, man. Stand up and see me now.

JACOB:
You beckon and . . . what heh?
(Jacob rises to his feet, surprised at the ease)
On my own two feet . . . I stand . . .

TIM:

Rise above the boards, sir; no more to bleed shame. You have poured enough of yourself into the cellars and soils below.

JACOB:
(Sputtering)
Sir? Is it I you address in such a gentlemanly manner? What say you? What can you mean by this?

TIM:

Have no ken, whom you address? Do you possess even the smallest notion? But of course, you don't. How would you? Encased here in this tomb, decade upon decade, counting the hours away with a paltry stack of coins, in tragic litany to all you wrought in life and were made to pay in death . . .

JACOB:

Oh, the hours, the minutes, the fragments of every moment! Every second ever passed in this horrific eternity is like the sharp, metal tooth of a clockwork. Cold slivers of coin tick away the time, and for all their toil, never a one has worn thinner for it, nor lost its callous sheen. These ghastly tokens are wicked talismans . . .

TIM:

. . . which will now lie fallow. Done. No more to be counted. You have counted long enough.

JACOB:
(Incredulous, afraid)
 I have counted . . . What . . . what are you saying?

TIM:

Mr. Marley, I am Tim, Tim Cratchit, son of Bob Cratchit, who was partner to the one you called partner in life, Ebenezer Scrooge, who links us over mystical planes and spiraling time, more so than any chain or creaking padlock ever could. Sir, I am the boy not only saved by Scrooge; I am the boy saved by you!

JACOB:

I? But long since gone was I, long set free from life's tentacled embrace!

TIM:

No, no, my good man. Your witless lethargy is but one aspect of your punishment! You have no conception, that what you accomplished on a Christmas night, nigh fourscore past, was the onset of a wave of good that became not only the salvation of one man, but of oh, so many, additional others. That we are all linked and part of a different chain you also fabricated, is as much a reality as was until now that monstrosity you yet wear.

JACOB:
(Lifting the lengths of chain)
These chains? I have borne them as I have suffered them. But you say: A chain? Unlike this thing?

TIM:
Indeed! The chain you alone transformed, Mr. Marley . .
.
JACOB:
Jacob. Call me Jacob.
(Sighing blissfully)

I have not heard my name spoken in so very long!

TIM:
Jacob, the chain you forged, and until this moment bore alone, so weighted with grievances, is now intertwined with the silver threads of progress and salvation!

(Tim pauses, taking stronger stance, for effect)

The chains of events you set into motion when you appeared to Ebenezer Scrooge on that fateful Christmas Eve accomplished so much more than the resurrection of a still-breathing soul. Your dramatic presentations set off a domino chain of good, which touched so very many!

You created apparitions and portrayed them as only Scrooge's one, true friend could. Who else would know all there was to know about Uncle Eb: The stories, the strife, the moments that mattered most? You showed him the way, Jacob. And in doing so, you paved the way for a multitude. You are one not to be shut away, but to be gathered up in an embrace of gratitude.

Thanks to your fantastical charade, a city block's worth of humankind benefitted, lived and thrived. Happiness was kindled. Healing was crafted, in heart as well as hearth. You built a wholly different kind of chain, Jacob. And it is this chain, by decree of the same nameless, formless ministers who directed your task those many Christmases ago, that guided me here tonight.

JACOB:
A good chain, then, a counterweight against these irons?

TIM:
A chain of Mankind, Jacob, linking hand to hand, thought to thought, word to deed . . .

JACOB:
Of imprisonment, then, no more?

TIM:
Quite the contrary.

(Tim guides Jacob to the darkened stage side, where the room gives way to the void)

Behold, Jacob Marley, visitations from a life so distant from your own, yet wholly linked back to you.

(Tim gestures to the darkened space beyond the room, which, as it is illuminated, becomes a window into Tim's own past, his life and accomplishments on Earth)

JACOB:
Sir, your words are music, each syllable a ray of light. You are among spirits an angel, and I unworthy of your presence. I am but a wretch, long ago joined ranks with the lowliest of shadows, not even granted leave to slink about the corners I occupied in life!
But for the one redeeming task of which you speak, have I dwelt in solitude and confinement.

TIM:
Oh, Jacob, know that angels appear in all shapes, all forms! On wingèd beings bathed in light, only the simpler mindset insists. Let us leave notions of halos and besparkled robes to a child's theater. Dark, dirty, and downtrodden are the true choirs, blessed, even if as ragtag suitors.

In their threadbare uniforms they scuttle about, and though they bring good to the world, they are barely tolerated, if not recoiled at, stepped upon and crushed, dismissed as nuisances, never venerated. The telltale wings many rather expect belong to grand altarpiece figures and fairy tale dreams.

Jacob, duly commanded, when given the task of redemptive consultation upon your lone and lonely friend, you served the mandates of your task. You knew well the life and times of one whose journey was in direst need of re-charting.

You, who in life parlayed the swaggering dandy, in death were not only the consummate actor, but also the tailor, stagehand, and director! You, Jacob, crafted a cast of characters that could blast apart a hardened man's stony hull and spark the soft matter that lay beneath, dormant, and underdeveloped.

You knew which lines to score, which scenes to play. You knew which words to speak; you knew just how in deathly silence to gesticulate. You, sir, in your wingless and earth-encrusted trappings, molded anew a man, long since fired into an impervious vessel of greed and selfishness.

And in doing so, you cracked open a fountainhead of giving that changed the lives of all who were also connected to my life. You changed me. I lived, I loved, I worked, and I played. Life was a grand and long affair for me. No, I did not die a child, as was foretold, Jacob Marley. I lived; and yes, because of you!

As such, the apparitions you conjured to show Scrooge his past, his present, and his future allow me now to show you shadows of another past; these from my own life, a wondrous journey, which end was celebrated less than a fortnight ago. Tears and laughter and embraces were my send-off, Jacob. . . Come, see!

(Vignettes are illuminated and enacted as Tim speaks, revealing moments in life that highlight his successes and happiest times: Vignette #1 depicts a graduation scene, where Tim delivers the commencement address, suggesting highest honors. The Cratchit family is in attendance, Tim's siblings now as adults. An old man stands with the family; it is the elderly Scrooge)

TIM
Witness, Jacob Marley, events that were, moments that live on, etched on the canvas of my history and in the memories of those I hold most dear, who shared these times with me as the very reasons behind any man's best hours of a life fully lived, of which I would not give up one high, one low, one sideways skewed aside, one diversion, or one correction.

There were achievements and testaments to learning and industry. I graduated with honors, my family in attendance to cheer me on, and good old Uncle Eb was right there as well, to shake my hand when I stepped off that dais. I was the first in my family to graduate from university, for as apprentice did my father rise in his trade. Through the generosity and faith of his employer, Uncle Eb, Father rose from untitled clerk to partner in a firm made venerable through honest trade and wise investment.

(The vignette progresses in scene and time)

My eighty years on this planet surged at full steam. I earned titles of husband and father, doctor, and professor. When not in the haven of my home, I chipped away at chemical and medical mysteries in laboratories, where many a long day and night were spent, developing devices that would change lives for the better. I had the honor to collaborate with a brilliant team of scientists in the eradication of the very disease that crippled my own childish limbs.

(Vignette #1 transforms into a different, much later commencement scene, with an elderly Tim presiding over the dedication of a hospital)

And then, at the waning seasons of my time on Earth, there came the dedication of a hospital, in honor of my life's work, to which I insisted the name Scrooge be also affixed over the entrance doors, in gratitude to my mentor, who was behind it all.

JACOB:
Why Tim, a great man among men you are! What indeed was wrought as the fruits of your labors! And I, in sorry contrast; what did I contribute to Mankind?

TIM:
Much, good sir. It was by grace of generosity that all this came to be: Grace as instigated by you; grace as personified in Uncle Eb.
(Muses, thoughtfully)
Although I must say, he always did give steadfast credit to some nameless collective known only to him, whom he affectionately called "his Spirits."

JACOB:
To think . . . all this, brought about by none other than my partner in life, Scrooge!

TIM:
Yes, Uncle Ebenezer, whose complete story I now at last see as you long saw it.
In this afterlife, I too share that transcendent perception, where Past, Present, and Future overlap to explain all the How's and Why's of everyone and everything we touched. I now also know the rest of your story.

Recall, Jacob, we are the sum of our deeds, which feather the finest and strongest of wings. Each good deed has the power to lift up its doer. And the best beauty? It lies in the fact that each sum of every Man can forevermore add onto itself. When most mortals think all is over and done with, there is yet a chance!

(Vignette #2 lights up to depict the next scenes in Tim's life, focused on love: Love between young adult Tim and the woman he would wed. The romantic encounter is transformed into a wedding scene. This scene transforms next into one in which Tim's wife presents him with his firstborn child. Tim, wife, and child are soon joined by other children to illustrate their growing family)

Jacob, there is more I wish to share with you . . .

(Vignette #2 concludes)

Uncle Eb's deeds in life still compound, and in their wake lies the simplest of sainthoods. Deification may remain unsung, but for the joys and successes of lives still affected by his past participation. To this day, sir, the time-travelling legacy that is Good knows no end.

And oh, how Uncle Eb fortified that legacy! It is a grand mansion that stands forever in his name. And ours. My children and their children are its keepers, and the great-grandchildren I knew only a brief time on Earth, whom I must now watch from afar, will keep its rooms alive for generations to come. For all this, dear Jacob, I thank you, for you are the one behind it all.

JACOB:
Such joy! Such a gift to behold! Would that the imbeciles to whose ranks I was called, had learned while we all still breathed . . .

Would that I could have walked abreast with the likes of you and met your outstretched hand as equal.

TIM:

I am no more or less than you, Jacob Marley. Such pedestal placing is to build a stand from which any human at one time must fall. Verily, Man tumbles farther the higher he builds. Let us set aside adulation as an error of habit sought by all who hunger for reward. Hapless others starve as all push through. . .

And who will scratch first at the banquet table? Paradise, Jacob, that place of plenty, is not about seating the choice few. If downcast eyes can be lifted to redemptive hope, our gazes will fall full upon the faces of each other in honesty and mutuality. We become peers and compatriots.

(Vignette #3 depicts a scene in which a mature Tim Cratchit is seated at the bedside of an aged Ebenezer Scrooge, who is near death)

TIM:
(Turns and in affection, touches Jacob on the arm)
As such, I look to you, squarely across the table, flawed and glorious in equal measure. Humans, being.

JACOB:
Oh, Tim, allow me this query, then. Dare I imagine the prayers of the dead can yet be heard?

TIM:
Know this, Jacob: There is and always has been an ear to receive every word ever uttered into the ether, where help was petitioned from the core of a heart, living or stilled. Your hoarse whispers were heard, and your effect upon Ebenezer Scrooge was noted.

JACOB:
(To himself, incredulously)
Oh, all my lamentations; that infernal recitation! I was heard! I was never as alone as I thought!

TIM:
Those saddest songs of all, indeed; their sound carries into the darkest recesses of the cosmos, where no reasoning mind could fathom an audience. Jacob, for Mankind to wrestle with his lot is but human. The dead walk in life amongst the living, whilst the living wander, like the dead. We are not needful of the Reaper's blade for to claim an end to the beating and bleating of a questioning heart.

JACOB:
And like I, countless are they with nothing but ice water in their veins, and cold, still pools where instead the fires of life should spark. This I know as one who lumbered for years as if through deepest snow.

TIM:
Even the most diluted of prayers, borne of nameless longing, can fly. One thousand practiced voices can call forth an ear, but so does the tuneless croak of a broken soul.

JACOB:
(Thinking back, sighing)
Would that similarly conjured spirits had come to me in some earlier incarnation, to haunt my night and set me aright while still a young man. What if they had visited me back when?

TIM:

You speak of spirits past? Of chance and intervention? Regret stokes fires that smolder and smoke and leave one to choke. Had you not toiled on behalf of Uncle Eb, what incalculable, unfortunate outcomes might have yet transpired? The ghosts manifested by your very ills resonated with the eloquence of a thousand lovelorn laureates! Pen or knife to tablet, however plundered and later rendered, your Spirits broke the chain of chains.

JACOB:

I suppose, the Spirits of Christmas Past, Present, and Yet to Come were as much of me as I am yet of them.
(The men walk over to Jacob's desk. Tim stirs the coins on his desk, picking up a few)

TIM:

As for your coins, and that counting and counting . . .

JACOB:

Have them! Take them! Throw them at the nearest altar! Oh, how as a young man I loathed the financial realm I was obliged to embrace!

TIM:

You wanted to serve your Muses and instead recite glorious lines of playwrights, who with quill and parchment filled pages with words that more truly spoke to your soul!

JACOB:

Princes and paupers, Romeos and oafs . . . a delightful soup! How I wished to live in life, I chanced to live in death. Imagine that!

TIM:

The duty that first tethers, later solders a man to his desk . . .

JACOB:

Aye, the desk became my anvil; profit became my prison . . .

TIM:

These coins, they were your subjects, tithes of a reluctant supplicant.

JACOB:

Awash with resentment, I took to the dark forces of angry ambition.

(Tim gathers up the coins into a bag or container of some sort. Jacob assists)

TIM:

Countless are they who, for wont of the luxury of free spiritedness, climb into saddles strapped to those most burdensome of horses, Obligation and Duty. Innumerable are they who trudge along rutted roads, rather than set expectation-laden angers afire with separatist dissent. Anger wrought of futility is a wicked plaything of the Fates, a binding and blinding force.

JACOB:
(Sighing sadly)
Far too many, I regret, are they who were dragged alongside my sufferings. This I understand with a regret that shines with painful sharpness. When I thought I acted the man, I was but a greedy and petulant aspirant.

TIM:
Your deeds of salvation for Uncle Eb are what now count. You labored with the lowliest of miners to find the bit of coal that could spark and warm a petrified heart.
My father, who suffered firsthand in the before, basked in the after, thanks to your endeavors. And the warming fire at the offices of Scrooge and Marley? In due time, the glow from their stove was joined by that of an army of brass-footed lamps, with light pouring forth from every window, illuminating the street and walkways in every direction!

JACOB:
(Laughing, shaking his head)
Those cursed, lumps of coal we hoarded. How cold we kept our offices! How like ice I recall even my own bed!

TIM:
Jacob, you turned those tides. You brought life in death, and joy in the dark face of fear. As Ghosts of Scrooge's life Past, Present, and Yet to Come, you transformed not only Uncle Eb, but also yourself.

JACOB:

Ah, the Ghosts of all Christmases were but the undertakings of a conceited, old coxcomb! The facades I employed in life served even better in death. What a trinity of spirited roles I played as their thespian deliverer. I am less an embodiment of Christmas Past, Present, or Yet to Come, than I am a grateful, if servile, puppet of a power far greater.

TIM:

Deliver, you did, Jacob. Your ghostly apparitions will forever be revered; and you, in exchange, will live forever more.

JACOB:

What is that you now say, Tim?

TIM:

The salvation of your friend and the lives he in turn touched, thanks to your great deed of that Christmas night, now direct a different outcome.

JACOB:

Pray, what are you saying?

TIM:

(Focusing directly on Jacob, with emphasis)
Jacob Marley, your penance is paid! You are square with the house.

JACOB:

Paid in full? You mean to say I am complete? Revelations and miracles!

TIM:
Your circle, sir, has come forthwith. And on the strength of that balanced scale, I have come here to carry out the one task with which I have been entrusted. A gift of grace I happen to possess, to give to a deserving other, and I am humbly graced to bestow . . .
(Placing his hands on Jacob's shoulders)
. . . a gift of after-life redemption . . . for you!

JACOB:
(Sinking back to his knees once more, looking up)
Tim! Tim Cratchit! Dare I believe my eyes, my ears? I know her beauteous name—dare I speak of—Hope?

TIM:
Dare, Jacob! Speak her name! Hope! Her sublime chords can harness the universe. Old chains, like yours, become dust in the face of Hope. Time and tithes collected through effort and endeavor outweigh any padlock, any stack of coins.

Being that Hope is everlasting, it is—and was—never too late.

JACOB:
Oh Lord in heaven! I cry! Such joy I feel! In death I have never felt so alive!

(Jacob rises. The men rejoice, embracing. Jacob's demeanor transforms, his entire form lifting up in confidence, reflecting the grace he realizes is his)

TIM:

In the names of all Spirits and Christmases that were, and ever will be, I place with you, Redemption. And your price, Jacob, duly paid, now requires we gather up. Up from here, and out, and far beyond. You need never look back.

JACOB:

Dear man, I accept this miraculous gift. I will place complete trust in you and call myself your humble recipient and ready apostle!

TIM:

Indeed! Your best journey has yet begun . . .

But first, Jacob, there is someone I want you to meet. Travelling companions make for a merrier journey.

End, Stave II

Stave Final

(Tim steps back from Jacob and walks to the door, which magically opens. An old man enters. It is Bob Cratchit. Tim takes his father by the arm and guides him over to Jacob)

TIM:
Father, may I present Jacob Marley. And Jacob, allow me to introduce you to my father, Robert Cratchit.

BOB:
Jacob Marley, sir, at last we meet!

(The men shake hands warmly, in greeting)

JACOB:
Mr. Cratchit! Partner and friend of my friend, I am honored to know you.

BOB:
And I you! And please, you must call me "Bob."

JACOB:
Though I do not know you, Bob, I know of you. I did live, so to speak, among you and yours, for a merry minute or two, a shadow against your walls on a Christmas Eve night long past. I was, with my former partner, an uninvited guest; and for that invasion, I must beg your forgiveness.

BOB:
Nay, forgiveness; there is to be none, for none is needed! A welcome shade you were! We are droll creatures, are we not? Rendering complex the simplest elements of our existence! I, for one, rejoice that you now too have the light of clarity to shine upon your books. When spirits hold aloft their torches, the better we all can see; but, sadly, generally, only long after the fact.

JACOB:
May one have half a match to shine as bright while still alive!

BOB:
Well then, in light of our timelines interwoven, I bid you welcome to our midst! Christmas is come again in the spirit of this moment, and so in the name of all furtive and ghostly guests, I say, "Bless you" and ask to call you, sir, "Friend."

(The two men shake hands again)

JACOB:
Bless you, sir. Friend it is!

(The two embrace. Jacob turns to address both men)

JACOB:
Aye, it is a strong potion in which this moment swims! A heady mead flows in my veins, and I can feel it—a warmth as real as anything I have ever felt!

BOB:
Ha ha! Good cheer, dear man, is infectious, and so it should be! Cheer flows not like a river, but a deluge! Soon enough, we shall drink our fill, partaking of the stories we will tell and the laughter we will share. Endless hours at our blithe disposal!

JACOB:
Aha, now this is how every story should end!

TIM:
And what's to say they do not?
(His demeanor and tone shift)
Jacob, our time is come. You will take your leave with us.

But, before we set off, there is one other to whom you must be presented, who has been appointed to serve, let's say, as a sort of chaperon. There is much to learn, leagues to recapture—so much has transpired! And who better to guide you than a compadre, an old soul, rather much like yours?

(A light approaches from offstage and comes to a stop at the closed door. Its rays spill over the floorboards from beneath the door)

BOB:
(As he takes Jacob by the elbow, turning their attention to the door)
Jacob, you, as I, know this person well.

JACOB:
(Realization setting in, incredulous)
No! Can it be? My heavens, is it . . .?

(Tim gestures towards the door, which opens once more of its own accord)

TIM:
Come, Jacob Marley; greet with me your friend.

(Tim walks over to the man who has just entered, an elderly fellow whose attire suggests he is an English gentleman from the mid-nineteenth century. It is Ebenezer Scrooge. Tim takes Scrooge's elbow and guides him over to Jacob)

(To Ebenezer, wryly)

Uncle; address once more your bit of undigested beef!
(Tim and Ebenezer embrace; then Ebenezer turns to Jacob. The two look upon each other in profound regard, joy visibly building between the two as recognition sets in)

EBENEZER:
Marley!

JACOB:
(Crying out in happiness)
I never…Ebenezer!

(The two men embrace)

EBENEZER:
Jacob . . . Jacob Marley!

JACOB:
In the flesh!
(Looks down at himself and laughs)
Ha! Well, what is left of him—however harvested, however undigested—stands here, once more, before you!

EBENEZER:
Nigh too much for this relic, however manifested, even after all these years!

JACOB:
Then, better named, "Old Blot!"

EBENEZER:
. . . or undone spud, you!
'twas but fear and pomposity that formed the words I sputtered!

JACOB:
Eb, you were most clever, even in terror!

EBENEZER:
Clever indeed! You reduced me, Old Blot, as was deserved, and well so! In life you were my partner; Jacob, in death you became my angel.

JACOB:
Eb, exalt me not, man. The gift of your presence renders my salvation complete. Speak no such titles! Call me Blot, call me Mustard, call me anything you like! Either which way, I am redeemed.

EBENEZER:
Well then, Jacob, blottiest and most grave friend, take my hand!

JACOB:
Ha! In gratitude!

(Ebenezer reaches out. Jacob takes his hand, pumping it madly. They hug once more, briefly, then step back a bit, beginning to laugh. Scrooge leans back dramatically to peruse Jacob, looking him up and down)

EBENEZER:
Well, well! You, thespian of the night, a dandy in life I always said of you, but as popinjay in death, you outdid yourself! The costuming that served in your youth but hinted at the wardrobes and wizardry you conjured up in the space of one glorious —and horrible, I might add— Christmas night!

JACOB:
I wailed with the best of them, eh, Scrooge? And so, my spirited trio met with your approval?

EBENEZER:
You were a spectacle among spectres! An inspired nightmare! The saints of the stage surely bow to you still! No ruthless banker, but it was as actor you should have embraced your citizen service.

You may recall, Marley, how in late hours together, when our ledgers were closed, and the ale flowed, and your surly guard was let down—what comical and affected speeches commenced from your jaws! The coins by day were nothing compared to the shouts of "Bravo!" that rained upon you when your night's endeavors were complete.

JACOB:
I tell you, the noggin throbs with the after-effects, even now. Worst of it, I can still recall those performances as we speak. What I boorish bore was I!

BOB:
(Laughing)
Your reputation precedes, you, sir, for, choice bits from your legendary diatribes were later oft quoted by Mr. Scrooge!

JACOB:
(Looks wryly at Scrooge)
You say?

TIM:
Indeed! Even I know a few of your famously colorful phrases.

JACOB:

Aye, yay, yay; would that I had haunted the festivities where those were the entertainment . . .

BOB:

. . . you would have seen our glasses raised to you at their conclusions!

JACOB:

(Wipes his brow dramatically and bows with a flourish)
Well, then, I am supremely relieved!

EBENEZER:

You know, Jacob, there was always the ruff of a ruffle about you, no matter how dank and dreary our offices remained in our years as partners.

Fortunes stashed otherwise found purchase in your colorful wardrobe. That, I remember clearly, but the finery was in service to none, especially as the wearer gained little joy from it, despite the investment, and most especially as the only audience was a dour company of one, who, unlike you, was born utterly bereft of a haberdasher's sensibilities!

JACOB:

(Remembering, wistfully)
A shallow satisfaction I took from my velvets and brocades. Oh, I spent fiendishly. It was, to say the least, a material weakness. I feathered my tail fit for the smuggest of peacocks.

EBENEZER:
(Shaking his head, remembering)
Aye, strut about you did . . .

JACOB:
(Paraphrasing Shakespeare, from King Lear*)*
Many a true word, spoken in jest!

EBENEZER:
In the end what good were those hoarded stacks of gold? Pharaoh's purses, dust-filled, weigh down the pockets of drifters who seek to make off with the riches buried alongside their boxed and wrapped keepers—and to what avail? The coin's potential, my dear fellow, evaporates like a last breath. Many have tried, but no farthing has yet to cross over, into the next realms.

Thanks to you, Jacob, and you, Tim, my wealth found purpose before it was too late.

TIM:
Riches are only rich if spent well. They are otherwise a costly and ripe cheese, gone bad.

BOB:
Aye, wise are ones who task their means to give joy, to heal, to build . . .

TIM:
Oh, one can grant the fashions of the day their due. . . Your costuming was as much a part of the story telling as were your ale-aided theatricalities.

JACOB:
Thank you, Tim. In context and suitable measure, why not?

EBENEZER:
Indeed, why not? Why walk the Earth a false pauper, only to be laid out flat, rich as a king?

JACOB:
And thank you, Ebenezer, for at least that. But truly, a clotted cream is a more honest rich. Lessons handed out; lessons taught. 'tis an agreeable wisdom for a trussed up, old ass!

EBENEZER:
You without fail always called a spade a spade, Jacob. And if ass you claim, then as one in the next stall over, I concede my supporting role. I was, and remain, your stubborn and steadfast kindred creature!

JACOB:
Always the flatterer, Scrooge, if a trifle more colorful than warranted! Your salty wit has not diminished with the decades!

EBENEZER:
You taught me well, Old Blot.

JACOB:
Teacher indeed! I steered you to near ruination! And for that I beg your forgiveness.

EBENEZER:
Forgiveness, Old Blot? No more of that! If we in our cojoined isolation wallowed as mortals, you were a friend, nonetheless.

And lone teacher? Mr. Marley, we choose as we walk, free-thinking fools and men. I embraced my accountability, so let us share in the reforms as both for us and of us.

JACOB:
Yes, you are right and wise; and it includes a forgiveness of self as well, does it not?

EBENEZER:
Yes, it does. So, our time now, Old Blot, will exist for us to rewrite our fresh sum totals, in tandem, thanks to the missive my dear ward, Tim, has delivered of you. Let us do this thing, look forward together. In joy. Enough of the woe!

JACOB:
What a weighty volume awaits transcription!

BOB:
. . . may it contain countless laughs!

TIM:
. . . and more of those verbose soliloquies!

JACOB:
Wait! I can feel baroque odes composing themselves as
I stand here. . .

EBENEZER:
Ah, and so hold onto them, good man; you'll outdo your
former Shakespearian self in droves! Henceforward, may
our partnership, reformed and reunited, include my
serving as rapt audience . . .

TIM:
And you must be sure to count us in!

JACOB:
Gentlemen, I am forever grateful. Thank . . .

EBENEZER:
(Jovially, interrupting)
 . . . then, in gushing gratitude we are even!

*(Ebenezer looks Jacob up and down once again, changing his tone
as he begins to lead Jacob to the wardrobe)*

But I must confess, mangy peacock, for all your frippery
of yore, to look upon you in this moment is to see but a
ghost of a ghost! We must find you a different coat,
something better befitting the pan-dimensional journey
of a ripe, old pair of resurrected cheeses.

JACOB:
(Sighing)
The Vanities were no more generous to me in the after
as they were in the before, Eb.

EBENEZER:
With fair countenance, neither one of us was overly blessed, but we had little need of looking glass idles, did we? You, Marley, may perhaps have had a slight edge on me there, with all those ensembles you'd concoct. . .

JACOB:
Oh, this figure once cut, tailored, and fitted to the nines, is now but a dull plow put to pasture. I am but an effluvium of rust and rot. And vanity? Ha! I am wizened with resigned recognition. On crumbs of humble pie I have scavenged and found them scrumptious!

EBENEZER:
Aye, the plumage in time was unceremoniously shed.

JACOB:
Indubitably—thoroughly!
(Resignedly, paraphrasing Shakespeare, from All's Well That Ends Well*)*
There was to be no kernel in this light nut . . .
(Tapping his forehead as he shakes his head)
 . . . the soul of this man was in his clothes.

EBENEZER:
Dear, fellow. We deserved no less than each other. Even our vanity was in vain! What a pair were we!
(Pausing, then gesturing to Jacob's garments)
And what about this? What is this molded, tattered thing you wear?

JACOB:
(Quoting Shakespeare, from Hamlet*)*
Aye! The apparel oft proclaims the man.

(Scrooge assists Jacob in the removal of his old coat)

EBENEZER:
No longer a corpse's coat for you! It has served its master and must remain here, as a rag to wipe the cobwebs we leave behind.

JACOB:
Farewell, old thing.
(To Scrooge)
Now, that will be a dust cloth for the ages!

(Jacob follows Scrooge in the direction of the wardrobe, but is abruptly halted, held by his shackles, the chain grown suddenly taut. Jacob cries out in pain and frustration)

EBENEZER:
First things first, Jacob. These shackles are no longer the fashion of the day . . .

(Ebenezer reaches into his pocket and withdraws an invisible key, which he turns in the air in the direction of the shackles. Magically, each shackle comes undone. The lid of the trunk lifts by itself. The shackles and length of chain are pulled offstage by unseen hands, slithering noisily up and into the trunk, swallowed into its depths. The trunk's lid slams shut)

JACOB:
(Lifting arms and legs, one by one)
Why, I feel as light as a feather!

EBENEZER:
Ha! Indeed, light as a feather

JACOB:
Lighter than a feather! I am a wisp of a snow cloud, a perch for a cherub!
(Dancing a few steps)
Oh Eb, a heavenly waltz calls to these brogues. I am as giddy as a schoolboy!

EBENEZER:
Ha, I know that step! It is a joyous dance, for it is carried out by the freest of wills.

JACOB:
Blessed freedom—a beauteous sentiment, my eloquent friend!

BOB:
Indeed, it holds the hearts and minds of Mankind aloft.

Tim:
(Patting his chest)
How true, Father. And, closer to heaven we are, with each recollection and protestation, holding Christmas in our hearts even here, with Uncle Eb's vow made manifest. What a power, happily and closely kept, like having the promised keys to Heaven's gates in one's very own breast pocket.

EBENEZER:
. . . with which we open those gates, and throw them wide, with starry mile-markers, not coins, to count along the way.

BOB:
Aye, we will count the riches of precious hours! What rolled around but once a year, Yuletides or Shrovetides or whatever—tides you'd please, will be rolled into one with the day!

JACOB:
Tides rolling . . .yes . . .by moonlight fueled. To make merry daily, what on Earth we could but once or twice a year set aside and celebrate? A delightful thought . . .

EBENEZER:
(Scrutinizing Jacob again)
Brother Yule, let us deal a moment longer with the issue at hand: That headgear—such might do to frighten an old codger as he takes his evening gruel, but it does nothing here but get in one's way . . .

(Ebenezer gestures to the bandage tied around Jacob's head. Jacob reaches up to untie the knot. Before his hands touch the fabric, the knot undoes itself, and the bandage is whisked up and off Marley's head and sails off, as if caught in a rippling wind. The men watch as the bandage flutters up and away, like a bird. Jacob is astonished but instantly grasps the happy magic of the moment. The bandage disappears. Jacob shifts his jaw back and forth, as if adjusting and loosening it up)

EBENEZER:
(Watching as the cloth flies away)
. . . who would have ever known a white and skittish head cloth to fly off like a bat, dotty as had it tumbled headfirst into Pan's bath?

JACOB:
(Waving farewell to the head cloth)
Cheerio, yon scrap! My creaking, leaking jaw is once more well bolted and oiled!
(Melodically)
Bah bah, bah; me, me me . . .
(Turning back to Ebenezer)
Oh, Scrooge, there is so much I want to tell you!

EBENEZER:
To be sure, there is much to share! Your jaw will be enthusiastically employed, and I promise to listen for millennia! Jacob, let us finish here and seek out a crackling fire and two chairs in some friendlier place.

JACOB:
Pray, if heaven is what we make of it, then might there be found, perhaps, a cup of warm broth?

(He shifts his jaw as if trying it out, gesturing as if drinking)
I might rather enjoy taking a sip of something warm . . . something nice . . . I have hungered for so long . . .

BOB:
Jacob, where we are bound, there are cups, nay, cauldrons of broth to thaw the creakiest of bones and joints!

TIM:
Gentlemen, our time is near! Let us head to the saltiest shores of the soupiest seas for the benefit of our famished brother. Cups of broth, cups of cheer. We will partake of it all!

JACOB:
This room . . . the floor, it gives way . . . the drapes, they grow thin like the mist . . .

TIM:
Yes, it dissipates before our very eyes. This room's tenure is over.

EBENEZER:
And its lone tenant shall at long last fly his coop.

TIM:
(Taking the lantern and lifting it up)
Onward ho, then, Captain and First Mates! Her Majesty's Ship the Cornucopic sails straightaway, for the spark of the log in the hearth, which bridges our horizons, crackles in welcome, and we, my fellow travellers, have a new sailor to instate!

(The men laugh)

BOB:
Friends, we must heed my son. All hands on deck!

EBENEZER:
Farewell, dark corners; with glad heart I lay claim to your resident! Marley, let our hearth find new harbour.

TIM:
Hoist the sails, ye hearties!

EBENEZER:
(Pausing, having noticed something amiss)

One moment, my dear Tim. Jacob; there is a final item that begs refurbishment. When on a Grand Tour of the constellations, a gentleman simply must be suitably garbed . . .

(Scrooge and Marley walk together to the wardrobe, whose doors magically open one last time. The costumes of the spirits of Christmas have now disappeared, and in their place is a fantastically lighted coat, a pair of shoes, and a hat. This reveal is a costuming high point. The coat can be as glorious and extraordinary—even comically so—as desired:

Imagine a jacket worthy of the court of Versailles, with patchwork pockets, kaleidoscopic buttons, and luminous lapels. Imagine a brilliantly contrasting, satin lining, and long coattails that writhe, animated, in eerily elegant flourishes. Imagine also, brocade shoes adorned with bells and gem-studded buckles, and a top hat with a brightly contrasting hatband, embellished with a sparkling sprig of holly.

Upon this reveal, Jacob stops, gasps, and expresses giddy delight. Scrooge appears shocked by what is revealed in the wardrobe and shakes his head, as if overcome with the garishness of the ensemble, to suggest it is far beyond anything he may have expected to find)

JACOB:
Oh my! What a glorious sight!

EBENEZER:
Mercy!

Jacob:
. . . in my days, I have never . . .

TIM:
Golly!

BOB:
Dear me!

TIM:
Uncle Eb, I now see you were true to your source. Your stories of Mr. Marley's—er—fashion statements were not in the least bit overdone!

JACOB:
. . . why, this
(*Sputters, overwhelmed*)
. . . is a fashion proclamation! I am agog! This ensemble . . . this, this masterpiece is . . .
(*Gushing, gesticulating*)
. . . is fit for the gods! Had every dream I had ever dreamt taken needle to thread in divine fabrication, this would have been their materialization!

EBENEZER:
My, but the powers of your imagination have but painfully outdone themselves!

JACOB:
Glorious—what a heavenly robe!

EBENEZER:
(*Laughing as he removes the coat from the wardrobe*)
How better to outfit a prodigal, old fop?

(Ebenezer and Bob help Jacob into his new coat. Jacob shucks his old shoes and dons the new ones. He preens and bows to the others in a humorous, theatrical display, who laughingly approve. Jacob places the hat atop his head and tips it to each one in turn, who return the gesture in playful deference)

JACOB:
(Striking a pose)
I am truly and wondrously arrived!

EBENEZER:
(Teasingly)
I should have guessed as much! Aye, the redemption of the soul may yet lack a crossing over into the salvation of good taste.

JACOB:
Shall I lay this coat down, sir, despite its pristine state? I will toss it as a rug over any puddle of mud that seeks to disrupt your path, if that is what is asked.

EBENEZER:
This prized goose, however newly feathered, is prepared to serve in most opposing roles!

JACOB:
(Flapping his wings)
At your service, Eb!

(All laugh together. The men make to raise invisible glasses, as if in a toast)

TIM:
(Interrupting the fun, with added urgency)

Uncle Ebenezer, Jacob, come now! When winter dawns, the spectral fire of the infant sun is there but a few, precious minutes. We must go now!

BOB:
Mr. Scrooge, Mr. Marley! The time is nigh; this room fades as we jest. The lighted portal is opened, and we must cross the hearthstone before the it is sealed off once more. Our stage will soon fail us, and the plane of this existence will be wiped clean.
(Emphatically)
We must be off!

EBENEZER:
Away then! Come, oh, trussèd one . . .

(Linking arms with Jacob, the two do a quick dance step together)
Look, Jacob! The suns are stars, and the stars are suns, and all point to one great light! Whatever we were, or may yet be, we are now passengers, and this, our winding sea.

JACOB:
(Stumbling)
Aye, what's this? I cannot keep a straight line! I am woozy of a sudden!

EBENEZER:
Good cheer, Old Blot, has gone straight to your head! Broth you will have soon enough, but the spirits have already infected you with their heady prescriptives! Aright yourself, man . . . keep new rhythm . . . you'll grow accustomed to the sensation soon enough . . .

(The men cannot resist; they quickly complete their make-believe toast, invisible glasses in hand)

BOB:
Here's to good cheer!

JACOB and EBENEZER:
Cheers to good cheer!

(Jacob stumbles again, just a little)

JACOB:
Well, joyously befuddled I hope forever to be, so please, forgive your stumbling comrade in arms!

EBENEZER:
Nonsense! Cheers, brothers and bumblers: Join ranks, fall in! Let us now away—you too, Sir Blot!

(The men toss their imaginary glasses over their shoulders with aplomb. Tim raises the lantern high over his head, which glows with renewed strength, now to illuminate their path to a new place of light and mirth)

TIM:
Away, mates! The Tides of Time beckon and so we cast off!

BOB
(Linking arms with Ebenezer who then links arms with Jacob)
Onward ho! Cheers one and all!

JACOB and EBENEZER:
Away! And Cheers! Away!

JACOB:
(Incredulous, sighing with happiness)
And to think; never to be alone again!
EBENEZER:
Ever again!

JACOB:
God bless it!

JACOB, TIM, EBENEZER, and BOB:
God bless us, all, and everyone!

(The group turns to face the back wall, which either slides away or is collapsed to expose a dark, limitless void, where at the center shines an almost blindingly bright and flickering light. It is to represent the Eternal Light, into which the men will presently disappear. The men begin to sing in unison the first stanza of the traditional carol, "I Saw Three Ships")

I saw three ships come sailing in,
On Christmas Day, on Christmas Day!
I saw three ships come sailing in,
On Christmas Day in the morning.

(Their voices fade as they walk into the light. As the men disappear from sight, swallowed by an ever-increasing darkness to suggest their receding into the far distance, the other cast members reappear on stage to complete the second and third stanzas of the carol.

The glowing flame of Tim's lantern, the last thing seen of the group, grows smaller and smaller until it appears to merge with the dazzling Eternal Light. After a moment of brilliance, the light is quickly extinguished, and it sinks into the ground, much like the winter sun on a low arc, when it slips beneath the horizon's edge.

At the moment the light disappears, snow begins to fall. Soft, pink-tinged illumination cast across the otherwise colorless backdrop suggests the sunrise is at hand. It is the first full day of winter; the longest night of the solstice has just passed.

A street scene quickly forms: Cast members dressed in wintery coats and gowns in festive colors of the season appear and move about, greeting each other as they sing. Perhaps a man carries an armload of Christmas wreaths; perhaps a youth carries a basket of bread, and in the other hand, he wrangles the carcass of a plump goose. Perhaps a few chorus members carry lengths of evergreen garland, which they begin to drape along a structure of some kind, perhaps a fence. A couple strolls arm in arm; a parent walks with their children. Youngsters run amongst the crowd, playing and laughing)

CHORUS:

And all the bells on earth shall ring,
On Christmas Day, on Christmas Day
And all the bells on earth shall ring
On Christmas Day in the morning.

And all the souls on earth shall sing,
On Christmas Day, on Christmas Day!

And all the souls on earth shall sing,
On Christmas Day in the morning.

(Curtain)

Epilogue

A Christmas Carol and *Jacob – A Denouement in One Act* are first and foremost ghost stories. It is their ghostly appeal that transcends their being pigeon-holed as only applicable to faith-based celebratory practitioners and their designated holidays. Good, old-fashioned hauntings find place in *all* story-telling traditions over time and are, therefore, to the delight of us all, organically all-inclusive. Not only that, *A Christmas Carol*, while being one of our best-loved Christmas classics, can also be construed as one of Science Fiction's most revered ancestors. Time travel, alternate universes, and diverging planes of existence are at the center of the hauntings Ebenezer witnessed and peripherally partook of, which, because they were all about exposing possibilities, continue to inspire new, tangential *Carol* interpretations.

Updated, ever-more garnished and darkly garish renditions appear with regularity; I'll stay tuned for a three-part series à la Back to the Future, with focus on alternate Dickensian netherworlds Yet to Come. . . And, while the *Denouement* helps bring home the tale of Jacob Marley, his story is equally as ripe for the fabrication of additional, other endings, beginnings, and more. Recognizing the parallels between Scrooge's and Marley's stories and all the Sci-Fi classics out there, potential outcomes prove limitless, for time and circumstance fly in every direction imaginable, leaving a thousand pieces of fabric to be whisked into the winds. What a brilliant folly of the Muses it was, who thought well to whisper as they did into Dickens' keen ears.

Thanks to the infinite nature of our universe, by logic, everything remains possible for us, too. As an ardent Arts supporter, I have long said: The Arts are a Bridge between Man and Mankind. They are a tangible, human link to one's Humanity. In that Spirit, allow me to bridge the imaginary planes of Marley's existence and share a "Yet to Come Part III;" or, in keeping with the structure, of Jacob—A Denouement in One Act:

Stave Final, Alternate Ending

(The men toss their imaginary glasses over their shoulders with aplomb. Tim raises the lantern high over his head, which glows with renewed strength, now to illuminate their path to a new place of light and mirth)

TIM:
Away, mates! The Tides of Time beckon and so we cast off!

BOB:
(Linking arms with Ebenezer who then links arms with Jacob)
Onward ho! Cheers one and all!

JACOB and EBENEZER:
Away! And Cheers! Away!

JACOB:
(Incredulous, sighing with happiness)
And to think; never to be alone again!

EBENEZER:
Ever again!

JACOB:
God bless it!

JACOB, TIM, EBEBEZER, and BOB:
God bless us, all, and everyone!

(The group turns to face the back wall, which either slides away or is collapsed to expose a dark, limitless void, where at the center shines an almost blindingly bright and flickering light. It is to represent the Eternal Light, into which the men will presently disappear. The men begin to sing in unison the first stanza of the traditional carol, "I Saw Three Ships")

> I saw three ships come sailing in,
> On Christmas Day, on Christmas Day!
> I saw three ships come sailing in,
> On Christmas Day in the morning.

(Their voices fade as they walk into the light. As the men disappear from sight, swallowed by an ever-increasing darkness to suggest their receding into the far distance, the other cast members reappear on stage to complete the second and third stanzas of the carol.

The glowing flame of Tim's lantern, the last thing seen of the group, grows smaller and smaller until it appears to merge with the dazzling Eternal Light. After a moment of brilliance, the light is quickly extinguished, and it sinks into the ground, much like the winter sun on a low arc, when it slips beneath the horizon's edge.

At the moment the light disappears, snow begins to fall. Soft, pink-tinged illumination cast across the otherwise colorless backdrop suggests the sunrise is at hand. It is the first full day of winter; the longest night of the solstice has just passed.

A street scene forms: Cast members appear onstage, whose faces and hands are cloaked in randomly assigned green or purple stocking knit fabric so as to eliminate any suggestion of race or gender identity. They are dressed in drab-colored, contemporary, rather unisex, wintery clothing. Every adult cast member is carrying a cell phone as they move about. Every gaze is fixed absently into the air or on the handheld devices. No one speaks to anyone or acknowledges anyone else's presence.

Two cast members walk together, perhaps with arms linked, as a couple. Another cast member carries large paper shopping bags, maybe also a fabric tote bag, slung over one arm. One cast member has a child in tow, which follows the adult with some reluctance, and in sullen silence. The child resists occasionally but is pulled along by the adult.

One cast member is engaged in a confrontational exchange over the phone and mouths their argument in silence as they stride across the stage. One adult is occupied taking selfies, making a display of themselves with their posing, clicking, and posting on their phone.

One adult reclines on the ground and holding a paper bag, from which a long-necked, glass bottle can be seen. This cast member appears to doze off, dropping the bottle to the ground. One adult crouches in a corner, holding a cup in one hand and a cardboard sign in the other. These two cast members are the only adult figures without cell phones. At one point, the cast member carrying the shopping bags pauses and sets them down on the ground. Another cast member suddenly appears, and dashes across the stage to grab the shopping bags, and to exit with them at the opposite side. The "shopper," engrossed in their phone, does not even notice the theft and soon continues on their way.

Next, a tall cast member appears onstage. He/she does not carry a cell phone. They look all around, repeatedly, with what appears to be great interest. This cast member carries a backpack. They pause towards stage right, and set their backpack on the ground, and then walk briskly offstage.

As this modern-day street scene unfolds, Ebenezer Scrooge and Jacob Marley will have walked slowly down a central aisle and will have come to a standstill directly in front of the stage. The men watch the street scene along with the audience.

As the modern-day street scene unfolds, and as the tall cast member sets their backpack on the ground and exits the scene, the two men turn to each other to speak)

EBENEZER:
Well, Old Blot, what say you? If we do this, we will need to step things up a bit.

JACOB:
A bit? Oh, Eb, I do not know. Where to begin? Where do we even start . . .?

(As the stage empties, Jacob and Ebenezer also exit to one side, shaking their heads. The stage goes dark. A spotlight zeroes in on the backpack, and soon goes dark as well)

(Curtain)

Conclusion

The book I discovered and somewhat clandestinely acquired at the Poet's Square in Berlin existed in my world for just over a couple decades, most of that time boxed and shelved, out of sight and mind. For a few years, the book, *Jacob—A Denouement in One Act,* shared space with other collectables in my home, tucked into the cubby of our massive dining room hutch. For a set of precious and studious hours, it resided on my kitchen table with salt and pepper shakers serving as paperweights to hold open the pages as I read well past many a midnight and entered every line and punctuation mark into an e-doc on my computer, doing my best to replicate its unique, slightly amateurish layout.

Here is what happened next:

It was on a Christmas Eve, about a month after I had completed my transcription of the *Denouement*. My daughter, our youngest, was the only child still at home with us, her older brothers being due to arrive the following day.

My daughter asked to set out a plate of cookies for Santa, as was our long-held tradition. Together, we arranged a few homemade spritz cookies on a cake plate. We placed them with a juice box onto a tray, along with a napkin, a straw, and an empty teacup per my daughter's logic that Santa would appreciate the dining accouterments.

On impulse, my daughter asked if I would allow my copy of *Jacob* to be placed on the tray alongside the snack, to create a pretty vignette and, as my daughter noted, to provide something for Santa to read as he rested and ate. Why not? I allowed my daughter to fetch the book from the hutch. Our little princess was soon after tucked into her bed and sound asleep.

My husband and I settled in with mugs of *Glühwein* (and those spritz cookies) to watch "It's a Wonderful Life," which was airing continuously on a Hollywood classics cable channel. Without realizing it, we sat through two runs of the movie, having dozed off toward the end of the first broadcast. It was well past midnight when we finally put our sleepy selves to bed.

What felt like two minutes later, it was Christmas Day morning. Our daughter, who alone among the three of us had the benefit of a full night's sleep, was bright-eyed and ready to go by 6 a.m.

My sleep-deprived husband, with his penchant for recording pretty much every darn thing our daughter has ever said or done, stumbled down the hall ahead of us with his camera and recorded the following exchange as she and I entered the living room, which appears below, verbatim:

My daughter: Oooh, so pretty! Mommy, Daddy, look at all the presents Santa brought us!

Me: *(Yawning)* Yes, honey, beautiful!

My daughter: And look, Mommy, Daddy; Santa ate all his cookies, and he drank his juice all up too!

My husband: *(Coughing)* Well, that was one hungry Santa!

Me: *(Rummaging lightly amongst the plate and napkin, lifting the tray)*

Wait, where is . . . Sweetie – big Sweetie – did you do something with the book?

My husband: Um, no. I thought you, er, Santa put it away last night, um, after he ate his treats. Yeah, after he went back up the chimney.

Me: No, I left everything as we set it up. *(Turning to my daughter)* Honey, did you do something with Mommy's little book of *Jacob*? Maybe you put it away? It's okay, you can tell me where it is.

My daughter: Nope, Mommy. I didn't do anything. Anyway, what book?

Me: What do you mean, Sweetie, "What book?"

My daughter: I dunno, Mommy. I just dunno about a book. I put cookies and juice out for Santa, that's all I did. Mom, Dad, can we open our presents now?

My husband: Of course, young lady.
(To me) Honey, we can look more in a bit. I'm sure it'll show up.

Me: *(Still looking around, puzzled, worried)* Yep, has to . . .
(To my daughter, sighing) Yes, honey, let's see what Santa brought . . .

I never saw "my" copy of *Jacob* again, nor did my daughter ever claim to understand what we had been discussing that morning. It was as if the book had never existed in her world. Had I not saved its text to an e-doc, which you, dear Reader, have now read too, I would have soon doubted if the *Denouement* had ever really existed in mine.

Looking back, the book's presence was indeed fleeting. It re-surfaced only occasionally from the depths and demands of my adult day-to-day, a fanciful distraction that, once finally tapped, also held a lovely lesson for me that I will keep in my own heart forever more. I remember my friend, Mary, telling me of a book of quotations that had inexplicably appeared on the floor of her sitting room some years ago.

A number of pages in the book, Mary said, had been annotated by none other than her late grandmother, who had been gone for decades. That book had also vanished, this one from a bedroom dresser top where Mary had placed it, right after she had read through its contents and come to understand its message and meaning. It was as if the book's task, once completed, mandated reclamation by the forces that had placed it there. I thought of both books – hers and mine – and wondered, as I still do:

How many other such volumes have randomly and mysteriously appeared to tell a story or open a window of new awareness, to help answer a question or resolve some issue, only to disappear soon afterwards, as if whisked away by unseen hands, when no one was looking? And if so, for what other purposes? For which other sets of eyes? And by what anonymous Angels or unnamed Spirits?

The End

115